When Sophie Gets Angry— Really, Really Angry...

When Sophie Gets Angry—
Really, Really Angry...

BY MOLLY BANG

SCHOLASTIC INC.

New York Toronto London Auckland Sydney
Mexico City New Delhi Hong Kong Buenos Aires

Sophie
was busy
playing
when...

...her sister grabbed Gorilla.

"No!" said Sophie.
"Yes!" said her mother.
"It _is_ her turn now,
Sophie."

Oh,
is Sophie
ever angry
now!

She
roars
a red,
red roar.

Sophie is a volcano,
ready to explode.

And when Sophie
gets angry—
really, really angry...

She runs and runs
and runs until she
can't run anymore.

Then,
for a little while,
she cries.

tweet

Now she sees the rocks,
the trees and ferns.
She hears a bird.

She comes to the
old beech tree.
She climbs.

She feels the breeze
blow her hair.
She watches the water
and the waves.

The wide world comforts her.

Sophie feels better now. She climbs back down...

...and heads for home.

The house is
warm and smells good.
Everyone is glad she's home.

And Sophie
isn't angry
anymore.

PURR

To all children, and to all moms and dads,
grandmothers and grandfathers, aunts and uncles and friends,
who ever get angry — even once.
M. B.

When Sophie gets angry, she runs out and
climbs her favorite tree.
Different people handle anger in different ways.

What do you do when you get angry?

This book was orginally published in hardcover
by the Blue Sky Press in 1999.

ISBN 0-439-21319-3

Copyright © 1999 by Molly Bang.
All rights reserved.
Published by Scholastic Inc.
SCHOLASTIC and associated logos are trademarks and/or
registered trademarks of Scholastic Inc.

21 20 19 18   5 6/0

Printed in the United States of America   09

First Scholastic paperback printing, March 2000